Prairie Dog Rescue

by Christine Ricci
illustrated by Ron Zalme

Ready-to-Read

SCHOLASTIC INC.

New York Toronto London Auckland Sydney
Mexico City New Delhi Hong Kong Buenos Aires

Based on the TV series *Nick Jr. Go, Diego, Go!*™ as seen on Nick Jr.®

No part of this publication may be reproduced, stored in a retrieval system, or transmitted in any form or by any means, electronic, mechanical, photocopying, recording, or otherwise, without written permission of the publisher. For information regarding permission, write to Simon Spotlight, an imprint of Simon & Schuster Children's Publishing Division, 1230 Avenue of the Americas, New York, NY 10020.

ISBN-13: 978-0-545-00477-0
ISBN-10: 0-545-00477-2

12 11 10 9 8 7 6 5 4 3 2 1   7 8 9 10 11 12/0

Printed in the U.S.A.

First Scholastic printing, September 2007

Hi! I am 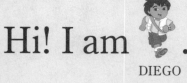.
DIEGO

I am on the prairie

with Mama and
PRAIRIE DOG

Papa .
PRAIRIE DOG

PRAIRIE DOGS live underground

in a .

BURROW

They can hide there if

they are in danger.

Oh, no!

I think I hear a !
COYOTE

are afraid of !
PRAIRIE DOGS   COYOTES

Mama 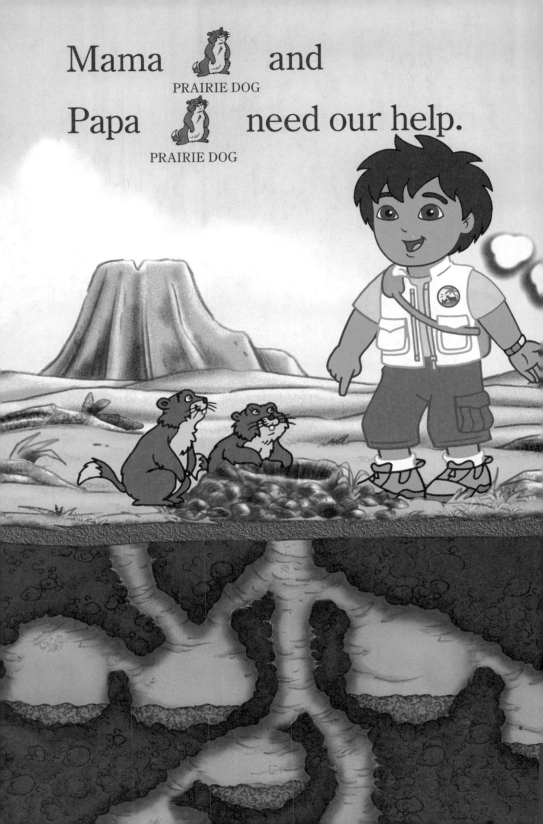 and

PRAIRIE DOG

Papa 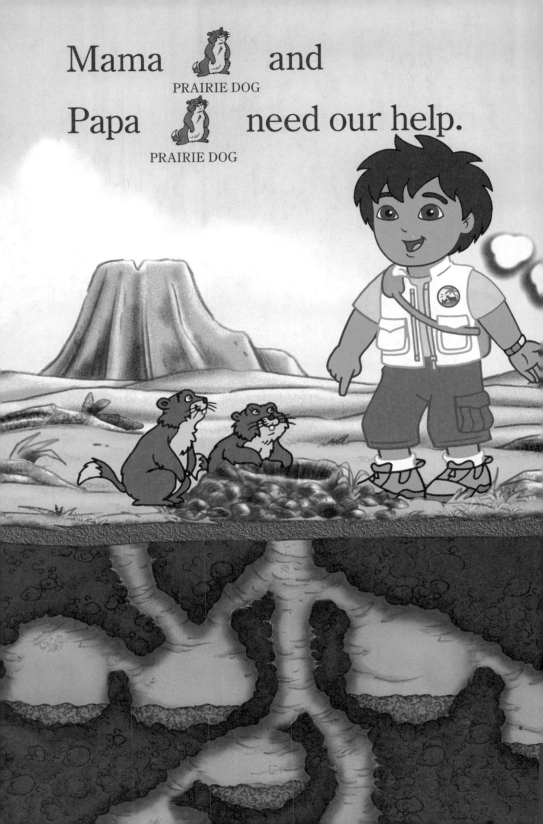 need our help.

PRAIRIE DOG

We have to get their five 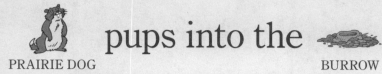 pups into the

PRAIRIE DOG   BURROW

to keep them safe from

the  .

COYOTE

There are lots of
animals on the prairie.
I see an and an .

ARMADILLO

OWL

Do you see any pups?

PRAIRIE DOG

Look! Two pups

PRAIRIE DOG

are eating .

GRASS

The is getting closer!
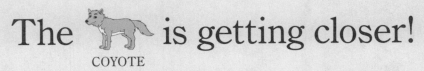
COYOTE

We need to find the other

 pups.

PRAIRIE DOG

We need to call them.

Say "Yip, yip!"
Two more pups

PRAIRIE DOG

heard our call.

They are jumping and

barking.

We need to carry the pups.

PRAIRIE DOG

My can turn

RESCUE PACK

into anything I need.

Should we use a ,
BOAT

, or a  to carry
SKIS   WAGON

the pups?
PRAIRIE DOG

Yes! A  !
WAGON

How many  pups
have we found?

PRAIRIE DOG

One, two, three, four.

We need to find five

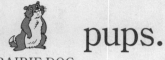 pups.

PRAIRIE DOG

One is still missing.

We need to use

my to look
SPOTTING SCOPE

for the last pup.
PRAIRIE DOG

Do you see him?

There he is!

Oh, no!

The 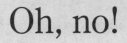 COYOTE is getting closer

to the  PRAIRIE DOG pup.

Which path should the pup take

to get to our ?

WAGON

Hooray!

We found all five

PRAIRIE DOG pups.

 **PRAIRIE DOGS** put a big pile

of  **DIRT** at their  **BURROW** so

they know where it is.

Do you see the biggest

pile of  **DIRT** ?

That is the  **BURROW** !

Mama  and

Papa
PRAIRIE DOG

are so happy to see all of

their  pups.
PRAIRIE DOG

Look!

Here comes the  !

COYOTE

We have to hurry.

All of the

PRAIRIE DOGS

are safe inside the .

BURROW

The is gone.

COYOTE

Rescue complete!